MISSING LUCY AT CHRISTMAS

Amish Romance

HANNAH MILLER

Tica House
Publishing

Sweet Romance that Delights and Enchants!

Personal Word from the Author

To My Dear Readers,

How exciting that you have chosen one of my books to read. Thank you! I am proud to now be part of the team of writers at Tica House Publishing who work joyfully to bring you stories of hope, faith, courage, and love.

Please feel free to contact me as I love to hear from my readers. I would like to personally invite you to sign up for updates and to become part of our **Exclusive Reader Club** —it's completely Free to join! Hope to see you there!

With love,

Hannah Miller

VISIT HERE to Join our Reader's Club and to Receive Tica House Updates:

https://amish.subscribemenow.com/

Chapter One

"How do you feel about it, Mary?" Anna Lapp asked her daughter, meeting her gaze across the dining table.

"About the job at the Friesen's farm?" Mary asked glumly. "I honestly don't have any feelings at all about it. Just like I have no feelings at all about anything since…"

"I know," Anna Lapp said patiently. "Since your sister… Since Lucy drowned. But, my child, it's time to stop blaming yourself for the tragedy. We've all been in mourning since last summer, but you have turned upon yourself it would seem, and you're too young to be giving up on life."

"I could've stopped her going out to swim in the lake," Mary said, her voice thick with remorse. "I could've prevented what happened."

"*Nee,* dear, you couldn't have prevented anything that happened, because it was the will of the *Gut* Lord above. Lucy ran off and jumped in the lake despite your repeated requests not to, *ain't so?* So how is this your fault? It's nobody's fault, Mary. We need to accept that perhaps it was Lucy's time to leave us, and now it's our duty to let go and remember her with joy – not constant sorrow."

"My life will never be the same," Mary declared firmly.

"I'm not suggesting it should be," Anna responded, not unkindly. "None of our lives are the same, are they? But your *daed* and I – and Becky, Sarah and Rachel - can't stand around and watch you go deeper and deeper into this depression you're in."

Mary dropped her head into her hands. "Thank you for trying to help me, *Mamm,*" she murmured. "But I don't think sending me away to work on someone else's farm is going to change anything. I've been working on our farm since last summer when Lucy...left us...and I haven't managed to stop thinking about her for hardly one minute."

"I know how close you both were. It's natural to miss your sister... but try to give yourself a chance. I have to admit that I hope the change of scenery will do you *gut.*"

"I s'pose you could say the Friesen's farm will provide a change of scenery, but I don't see how looking after their animals while they're away is going to help."

"It's only for a short while, daughter, so it's worth a try," Anna said gently.

"I guess," Mary said. "The Friesens are Mennonites and you know I'm not that familiar with their ways."

Mary's father, Jacob, who had been listening quietly to this interchange, spoke up. "The Mennonites ain't so different from us," he said. "They are just a little more lenient in their ways than we are, with cars and using electricity. Besides, the Friesens will be away visiting their family in Pennsylvania, which is why they need someone to take care of their animals. You won't have much to do with them."

"So, I'm going to be there all by myself?" Mary asked. "Will I be even home for Christmas?"

"Of course, you'll be home for Christmas. Your sisters will also visit you regularly," her mother said. "And it's not forever. This is just to give you a break from things here."

Mary pushed her chair back and got up from the dining table. "Well, I s'pose I should go and pack my things."

Anna and Jacob looked at each other as Mary exited the room.

"She's eighteen years old," Anna remarked, "and seems to have given up on life already. Are you sure it's all right for her to be alone at the Friesen's farm?"

"It's the only way I could think of to help her snap out of her current state of mind," Jacob replied. "The moment I heard about the job, I felt like it might be something until other opportunities open up."

Anna sighed. "She used to make the most beautiful quilts but hasn't put so much as a stitch into a piece of fabric since our dear Lucy left us. Otherwise, I might have suggested she open a little shop to sell her work."

Up in her bedroom, Mary stood bleakly surveying the contents of her suitcase and felt like she was being sent into exile. The suitcase looked empty with her one grey and two blue dresses, some *kapps,* a shawl and writing materials. In her mind, she could hear her parents conversing. She seemed to be the topic of conversation a lot these days. Initially, they had let her mourn Lucy's death without interfering because they were equally devastated. But when her parents and sisters appeared to have come to terms with their loss, and she was still submerged in guilt and pain, there had been a shift in her family's attitude, and their anxiety became more apparent.

"I don't want to go away," Mary said aloud.

"Mary," her mother said, coming into the room clutching an assortment of jars in her arms. "I thought you might like to take some homemade preserves with you."

Mary stared at the jars that her mother was piling into her suitcase without waiting for an answer as to whether she wanted them or not.

"Surely, I'm not going away for *that* long, am I?" she asked, looking troubled.

"Of course not," Anna replied. "I just want you to take a little taste of home with you."

Anna burst into tears and threw her arms around her daughter. "Oh Mary, Mary," she said. "I know how you feel. We all have felt the same, but you just need to let it go and try to move forward."

"Are you punishing me because I can't forget my own sister?" Mary asked, tears prickling her eyes.

"*Nee.* We're merely trying to help, that's all," Anna replied. She hugged her daughter again. "This is hard for me too, you know, but your *daed* gave the Friesens his word. We'll come around and visit you, so you don't have to feel like you're completely on your own."

Mary dried her tears and looked up at her mother. "I know you will," she said. "It's not that far away."

Chapter Two

"Have you got a shawl for the ride to the Friesen's farm, Mary?" her sister Becky asked.

"*Jah*, I do, thanks Becky," Mary replied. "I've worn some warm socks, too."

"We'll miss you," Sarah whispered as she hugged her sister. "But it's not as if you're so far away that we can't come and visit you as often as we can get away from our chores."

"We'll have more chores now that you're not here," Rachel remarked with a laugh. "You always help with ours."

"I'll be back before you know it," Mary replied stoically.

"Come on, now," Jacob urged. "We've got to get to the Friesen's farm before they leave."

Mary turned to wave to her family, and then climbed into the buggy beside her father. She didn't turn around as they drove away, and instead fixed her gaze on the scenic winter landscape. She shielded herself against the chilly breeze by drawing her shawl up over the back of her head like a hood.

As they drove out of Cedarwood Village and headed toward Dovetail Glen, Mary made an attempt to ignore her growing apprehensions; trying to focus instead on thinking of her time away as a much-needed adventure.

"There's only a note stuck on the door," Mary said, her anxiety growing.

Jacob snatched the paper off its nail and squinted at the writing. He chewed on his lower lip thoughtfully. "This is strange," he said, as Mary leaned across her father's arm to read the scrawled message.

Dear Mr. Lapp,

We're terribly sorry we aren't here to greet your daughter and settle her in. We had to leave a day earlier for Pennsylvania. There are supplies in the pantry, and we hope that Mary will make herself comfortable. Thank you so much for helping us out at this time when we needed to rush off earlier than planned.

P.S. The key is under the flowerpot to the right of the front step.

"Hmm," Jacob grunted, as Mary got down on her knees to retrieve the key and unlock the door.

"It's a nice house," Jacob observed, looking around, "but I would have been sure to put in a bigger porch."

"This is nice too – just one step up to the door, and a fenced-in garden. Of course, the plants have been overcome by the winter cold, but there is an evergreen standing," Mary remarked.

"It looks deceptively small, this property," Jacob said, "but the farm stretches out behind the house... and there are stables, a dairy shed and chicken coop to the side."

"You've been here before," Mary said.

"I have. Several times. I've been coming by this farm for some months now. They are good people, the Friesens."

"I hope I'll be able to manage all the work single-handedly," Mary murmured.

"They've downsized a lot, recently, and just have a horse, two cows and some chickens," Jacob replied. "Rumor has it that they might go away permanently to Pennsylvania at some point."

Mary looked around her. They had entered the living room,

which was compact and cozy, with a fireplace and a comfortable-looking sofa.

"This way, Mary," Jacob said, leading her through the door on the left of the living room. "This is where the dining room and kitchen are."

"Where do I stay, *Daed*? I do hope they've arranged a room for me," Mary said, looking around for more doors and finding none, except a back door leading out of a washroom.

"This way," Jacob said. "Follow me."

He led Mary back into the living room, and Mary saw a narrow staircase leading to the upper floor of the house.

"Your room is up here," Jacob said, climbing up the stairs and waiting for Mary on the landing. "Here," he said, pointing to a door on the right. "The missus told me she'd put you in here."

"It's very nice," Mary declared after pushing through the door, taking in the dresser with a mirror, and the bed with a patchwork quilt on it.

"But where are the lanterns?" she asked.

Jacob smiled. "There are none."

Mary's eyebrows shot up when Jacob reached out and turned a light switch on.

"Oh my," Mary exclaimed. "I forgot. I don't know if I'm comfortable with this."

"You will get used to it, daughter. And it's only for a while," Jacob remarked. "If you really don't want to use the electricity, I can bring over some lanterns. But I do think you'll be fine."

"How long is 'only for a while'?"

"Well, the Friesens didn't give us a precise date when they'd be back – mainly because they are going to take care of an elderly relative through December," Jacob replied.

"Am I to be here alone the whole time?"

"If you can't manage, Mary, we can send Becky or Sarah to keep you company," Jacob reassured her.

After her father left, Mary hung her clothes in the closet and put her suitcase away. Then she went outside through the back door to look for the animals. She almost collided with a portly gentleman while going in to check on the horse.

"Oh, *gute mariye*, miss," the man greeted her as he tipped his hat.

"*Gute mariye*," Mary returned the greeting. "You couldn't be Mr. Friesen, could you?"

The man chuckled. "Oh no, miss," he said. "I'm James Zook, a neighbor. The Friesens asked me to take care of their animals until you arrived. You are Mary Lapp, *ain't so?*"

"I am, indeed," Mary replied. "The Friesens left a note saying they had to leave a day early. Is everything all right with them?"

"Not too sure, Miss," James answered. "They just gave me a call and asked me if I'd help out with the animals for a day."

"Your farm must be close by," Mary said, feeling comforted at having other Amish people living in the vicinity.

James Zook chuckled again. "My farm is about a thirty-minute buggy ride away, so I'm not within hollering distance."

"You said that the Friesens gave you a call...?" Mary asked.

James Zook guffawed. "I'm sorry, Miss, I meant a call...on the phone. Of course, they have a phone in their house," he explained.

"Oh," Mary murmured. She looked around the stable where they were standing and went up to the horse – putting out a hand to stroke its mane.

"You fond of horses?" James asked her.

"I'm fond of all animals. Grew up around them. My sister Lucy and I..."

Her voice trailed off and she felt the familiar lump in her throat.

James Zook coughed. "Well, Miss, if you'd come along with me, I'll just show you around to the cows and the chicken coop, and then I'll be on my way. I'll also leave you our number in case you need anything. You can leave a message for me."

"I'm sure I won't be needing anything," she blurted out.

"Well, if you do, just use their phone. It's in the living room. I'm sure you'll find it easy enough."

Mary shook her head. "If it's all right with you, I would be happier not using their phone." She shifted uncomfortably. She wasn't sure she was going to like it here with all these fancy things. "In fact, I... Well, if you would be so kind as to let me know where I may find some lanterns, I would be most grateful."

"Lanterns? Don't think they got any round here. You have electricity while you're here," James Zook remarked.

"I know," Mary replied. "But that doesn't mean I have to use it, does it?"

James Zook gave Mary a curious look. "Well now, most in your position would be eager to use these modern conveniences, but I respect your decision to abide by your beliefs. And I'll be happy to come by in an hour or two with some lanterns for you to use."

"You're very kind," Mary said. She looked curiously at him. "Mr. Zook, may I ask you a question? I think I might be mistaken about something."

"Go ahead," James Zook said.

"Are you a...ummm...Mennonite?" Mary asked. She figured he must be by the way he'd been talking about phones.

James Zook nodded. "I am indeed," he answered. "And we're really two sides of the same coin, in many ways."

So, he wasn't Amish. His clothes made him appear so, but she'd been wrong.

"Please, call me Mary," Mary said. "And thank you for showing me around. I really appreciate it. To be honest, I was nervous when I found that the Friesens had already left."

"Well, if you need anything at all, my wife Susan and I will be happy to help. After all, what are neighbors for?"

Mary gave him a grateful smile. "Thank you, Mr. Zook."

"Now, here's my number," James Zook said firmly, taking out a pen and pad and scribbling on a piece of paper. "Keep it...and call if you ever need anything."

Mary accepted the phone number because James Zook was so kind and helpful, but the moment he left in his buggy, she tore up the piece of paper and consigned it to the trash can by the side of the house. Then she went inside and stood staring at the telephone when she jumped at a sound behind her.

"Oh my!" she exclaimed at the sight of a large, furry, black and white cat with arresting green eyes. "Where did you come from?"

The cat mewed in reply and strolled over to a dish of cat food that Mary noticed lying near the living room. As she stood staring at the fluffy animal, unused to seeing a cat in the main house instead of being confined to the barn outside, she heard a shrill ringing, and jumped again. It was the telephone.

Mary stood still and gaped at the device. The ringing stopped and a long beep preceded the sound of a woman talking.

"Hi Mary, we're so sorry we weren't there to settle you in," the voice said. *"I'm Lydia Friesen here, calling to say that Fluffy the cat needs taking care of as well. We omitted leaving instructions about him. You just need to put out a saucer of milk for him in the morning and use the cat food in the kitchen the rest of the time. If you pour some into a bowl, he will eat it throughout the day whenever he's hungry. If you need any information about where to find things, please feel free to call. Bye for now."*

Mary looked from the phone to the cat who was calmly eating his meal and then went into the kitchen to search for the cat food. She found a large bag with an unrealistic picture of a smiling cat lying on a shelf and took it down to examine it; wrinkling her nostrils at the pungent odor that emanated from the bag.

She knew that cats liked fish, and that's what they fed theirs —although it mostly fed on mice. She decided to make a trip to the market, at some point, to buy some fish for Fluffy. It was still early in the day, and as James Zook had done the chores for the morning, and she had little to do, Mary began to explore the premises.

She saw the barn by the stables and went inside. It was clean and neat, with sacks of grain methodically stacked, some crates of apples and various farm implements. There was also a bicycle, and Mary hopped on and took a little ride around the barn to see if it was in working order.

She would ask James Zook where the nearest market was when he returned. She had found some food in a refrigerator earlier, but it wouldn't last forever, so she decided to buy herself some groceries as well as some fish for Fluffy.

She was wheeling the bicycle out of the barn, when James Zook returned with two lanterns and half a dozen oil lamps.

"This was all I could find," he said, carrying the lanterns and lamps into the house for her, as she parked the bicycle.

"Oh, thank you so much," Mary told him. "I will feel far more comfortable having those in the house rather than all those bright electric lights."

James Zook eyed the bicycle curiously. "Going somewhere?"

"*Jah*," Mary replied. "I thought I'd visit the market to buy some supplies. I thought I'd buy a few more grocery items and maybe something special for the cat."

James Zook chuckled. "It will take you a while to reach

Dovetail market on that bicycle, Mary, so perhaps you'd be better off letting me drive you there in my car."

"That's kind of you. But won't I be taking up too much of your time?" She had some reservations about going with him in his car, but then plenty of folks in her district hired drivers to take them longer distances.

"I don't mind at all," James Zook said. "But I suggest we go tomorrow. Unless you don't have anything at all to whip up for a meal today."

"I'll check the chicken coop for eggs," Mary replied, "and perhaps bake some biscuits."

Chapter Three

As James Zook prepared to leave, Mary called out for him to wait. "Mr. Zook, which direction is the market? I might actually cycle there sometime. I could use the exercise. But even if I don't go, it would be nice to know where it is exactly."

"A few miles south of here," James Zook replied. "And I still recommend that you let me and the missus take you tomorrow. It's downright cold out here."

"A few miles? That's it?" Mary laughed. "That's not far at all. I ride longer distances all the time."

"Well, check that the bicycle has a lamp, as it gets dark quite quickly these days," he cautioned her.

"I will be sure to check the lamp."

She went back inside and locked the door. Despite Mr. Zook's misgivings, she bundled up thoroughly against the cold air, hopped on the bicycle, and pedaled away in the direction he had indicated. Sometime later and without much trouble, she found the market. It seemed to be the hub of Dovetail Village. It was small and friendly, and Mary felt her spirits lift. Somewhat wryly, she realized that she'd been so involved with learning about the Friesen's home and animals, that she hadn't had much time to wallow in her misery over Lucy's untimely death.

She wandered through Dovetail Market, looking for the groceries she needed, and to her relief, she also found some fresh fish on sale. She bought a bit for Fluffy, and then headed back to the Friesen's farm with her bicycle weighed down with her shopping. Regardless of the extra weight, she made swift progress and was back at the house in time for a late lunch.

Fluffy could smell the fish the moment Mary arrived and refused to give her time to clean or cook it; mewing at the top of his voice until she gave it to him on the kitchen steps. Soon, all that was left were some scales and a bit of fish tail, which Mary scooped up and dropped into the trash. It was while she was engaged in this task that she had the strangest sensation of being watched. This was not something she'd ever experienced before, so she tried her best to shrug off the feeling, but it returned each time she stepped outside.

"I think I'm going to have my meal now, Fluffy," Mary

informed the cat, and set about roasting the meat she had bought and baking some biscuits to go with it. She sautéed some vegetables in a cast-iron pan and then sat down to eat at the kitchen table.

A light breeze blew into the room from the back door, which she realized she hadn't closed securely. She rose to close the door more carefully, when she had the same sensation of being watched. She shivered, and tried to shake the sensation off, but it persisted. The kitchen window, though closed, had clear glass panes that anybody outside could look through. Mary got up swiftly and drew the curtains across the window and then, feeling more than a little unsettled, she finished her meal.

Soon it was time to go out and check on the chickens and make sure they were all shooed into their shelter for the night. She then went to check on the horse and the cows. An automatic light by the stables popped on, and Mary was glad of the illumination once the darkness fell—even if the light was provided by electricity.

Back inside, she bolted the front door and the kitchen door and lit the oil lamps instead of turning on the lights. Then she made herself a cup of hot chocolate. As she sipped on the warm liquid, memories of Lucy returned to torment her, and Mary found her thoughts once again revolving around her regret and self-recrimination over her sister's death.

Restless now, she got up and wandered around the empty

house, relieved that she had the space to grieve without someone telling her to snap out of it, and she allowed her tears to fall.

By the time she was ready for bed, she was exhausted. She had barely gotten under the warm quilt before she fell fast asleep.

Sometime in the middle of the night, Mary realized there was a warm furry body on her bed, and in the lamplight which she'd left burning low, she saw Fluffy. She didn't know how she felt about sleeping in a bed with a cat, but she supposed Fluffy was company after all.

It was just past midnight, when Mary thought she heard the sound of a door banging in one of the outbuildings. She went to the window and peeked out from behind the curtain. In the light of the moon, she imagined she saw the barn door shudder to a close, and her hair all but stood on end. She began to pray for safety as she padded back to bed and slid under the quilt.

Fluffy curled up next to her, and though she hadn't been in favor of sleeping in such close proximity to any animal, she was grateful for the company. That night her dreams were more dramatic − with doors opening to reveal strange shady forms. She awoke at dawn afraid to go about her chores, but she wouldn't coddle herself. So, she washed, dressed, said her prayers, and then went down to the kitchen and set out her breakfast makings. She braced herself and stepped outside, armed with a few hastily gathered rocks in her fist, and her shawl about her shoulders.

She was milking one of the cows when she heard something like scuffling in the nearby shed, and a small thud. She froze on the milking stool and the cow tensed, but Mary resumed milking and kept up a steady flow of prayers as she did so.

Before the sun broke through the clouds, Mary went to groom the horse and fill its water trough, holding a lantern aloft to light her way.

"You're out of grain," she said to the horse as it whinnied. "Wait a minute, and I'll fetch some."

She remembered seeing neatly stacked grain sacks, and hesitantly set off to fill her bucket, still holding the lantern high, but tensing at the memory of the door opening and closing at night.

"Just my imagination," she murmured to herself, moving more purposefully toward the back of the barn. She hesitated before she went further back into the shadows. Once there, she set the lantern down and swiftly filled the bucket with grain, leaving the lantern on the floor since she needed both hands free to carry the heavy container to the stall.

"Eat up, my friend," Mary said, pouring the grain into the horse's feeding trough. Then she returned to the back of the barn to fetch her lantern. When she walked back, however, she had the same sensation of being watched as she'd had the previous day, so she rushed and picked the lantern up, just as an apple rolled out of an overturned crate.

Mary stopped short and froze. The crates had been neatly stacked the previous day, but now one of them was overturned.

"It could be a barn cat...or another night creature," Mary murmured to herself, setting the lantern down again. She resolutely walked to the crates to set them right—one atop the other. She took a few apples to bake a pie and, on an impulse, counted the ones that remained in the top crate – and left the barn. She wished she could lock the barn door, but it wasn't set up that way, and Mary couldn't see that there was any way of locking it.

She returned to the cow for the pail of milk and walked briskly back to the house with it, bolting the kitchen door behind her. As she set the pail of milk on the kitchen counter and bent down to get the griddle from the bottom drawer of the oven, a thought struck her, and she straightened up again to stare into the pail of milk.

The level appeared to have gone down a notch – barely discernible, but Mary had sharp eyes. Hoping she was imagining things, she put all her attention into plopping a square of butter into the skillet and scrambling some eggs while heating up a cup of milk for some hot chocolate.

There was a certain charm to having breakfast alone and

eating whatever she fancied. Dovetail Market had supplied her with bacon as well, and she tossed a few strips in the pan after her eggs were done. Then she sat down to eat, with the curtains of one window opened, so she could look out at the landscape before her. When the sensation of being watched through the panes became disturbing again, Mary drew the curtains and resumed her meal.

Goodness, but she was becoming a scaredy-cat. She never thought of herself in those terms, but then, she'd never been on her own for more than an hour or two before, either.

After breakfast, she cleaned the house – glad to find an old-fashioned broom amidst the clutter of more modern cleaning apparatus. As she swept the floors and dusted the furniture, Mary's thoughts returned to Lucy again. The familiar memories returned, with the all the self-recrimination, and regret that she hadn't watched her younger sister more closely on that fateful summer day.

"Why did you have to run off to the lake, Lucy?" Mary asked for the millionth time. "And why do these memories return to haunt me every single day? I can't live like this."

She found herself praying that soon she would be able to think of Lucy with joy and peace. And that perhaps, she could believe that what had happened had been the will of God, after all.

Fluffy kept Mary company through the whole process of cleaning but backed away when Mary began to wash her clothes.

"Don't like water, do you?" Mary queried, as the cat hurriedly ran off. The Friesens had a dish-washing machine, but Mary wasn't going to use it, nor could she. She had no idea how to work the thing or how much of the detergent to put in.

She decided to hand rinse her few dirty underthings from the day before. She put the plug into the bathtub and used it to do her laundry. Afterward, she took the clothes out into the backyard where she had spotted a clothesline the day before. She began to hang out her garments to dry. Even though the temperatures were low, she knew the clothes would dry—even if they froze solid first.

She stole a glance at the stables and the barn, but nothing seemed amiss. The feeling of being watched, however, remained, and then it intensified, as Mary began to chop some wood for the fireplace in the living room.

When she was arranging the logs in the grate, Mary heard the sound of fierce squawking from the chicken coop and ran out of the back door to check on it; with one of the smaller logs in her hand. When she reached the coop, the chickens were running about, completely disturbed. Mary frowned, when she spied a broken egg by the entrance of the coop, and kneeling down in the dust, she checked for footprints. *Ach,* but she hoped it wasn't a raccoon. Once that started, she'd never get another egg.

She didn't see any signs of an intruder, however, so she cleaned up the broken egg and disposed of it, leaving the coop once the chickens had settled.

Chapter Four

Toward noon, the welcome sound of a buggy brought Mary to the front door, and she almost whooped with joy to see Becky and Sarah alight.

"Becky! Sarah!" she exclaimed, rushing towards them. "Am I glad to see you."

"*Daed* let us drive here on our own," Sarah said excitedly, as Mary led them into the house.

"Provided we don't stay too long...because we have tons of work to get back to," Becky added, sitting down on a sofa.

"How is *Daed*? And *Mamm*?" Mary asked, her eyes misting over, even though it had only been a day since she had seen them.

"They miss you, I can tell," Becky replied. "We all do."

"I feel like I've been banished," Mary remarked with a wry laugh.

"Actually, I envy you being in a lovely farmhouse like this on your own," Sarah declared, glancing around with appreciation. "With electricity and everything."

"I don't use it," Mary replied. "I have lanterns instead – like at home. And honestly, being on my own isn't that much fun, and well, it can be scary."

"Scary?" Sarah asked. "What do you mean?"

"I've heard strange sounds – and things have been happening. Like the milk level in the pail this morning was lower after I left the pail unattended for a bit. And I found a broken egg in the chicken coop after the hens went into a frenzy. I also found a crate of apples overturned...after I heard a door outside open and close during the night."

Sarah and Becky exchanged glances, and then Becky turned to Mary and gently said, "You could be imagining things, you know."

"I saw the look you two gave each other," Mary said, annoyed. "You all think I'm going crazy...but I'm not. I know what I saw and heard. I even feel like I'm being watched. That's the worst feeling of all."

Sarah laid a comforting hand on her sister's shoulder. "You've been through an awful year, Mary. We all have. And Christmas is coming, which makes it worse..." She paused for a moment and then went on. "All that you just described seems to me to be just, well, your imagination. I think your thoughts are getting twisted."

"Twisted?" Mary repeated. "What does that even mean?"

"I'm sorry, dear Mary," Sarah replied. "You did mention that you felt like you were being watched. Maybe, it's the guilt you've been experiencing because you blame yourself for Lucy's death."

After her sisters had left, Mary thought long and hard about what Sarah had said. Her remark about being twisted had cut deep, and Mary wondered if her guilt was indeed showing itself into some sort of paranoia. She prayed in earnest that she was not losing her mind.

It was early evening when Mary heard the crunch of gravel in the drive again, and she opened the door eagerly, hoping to see her parents. But it was James Zook and his wife, Susan.

"Come inside," Mary said, inviting them in.

Susan Zook held out the pot she was cradling carefully in her arms. "This is some stew for you, Mary," she said. "Made with fresh meat and vegetables, too." She smiled indulgently. "James told me you didn't have much on hand, and we can't have that, now, can we? I myself like growing my own vegetables and we rear our own livestock as well, so I thought this stew was just the ticket."

"And she runs in to the market almost every other day to buy things we need, so she can advise you on what's available," James added.

"Thank you for the stew," Mary said, lifting the lid and sniffing at the contents appreciatively. "But I can't eat all of this on my own, so why don't you join me?"

"We should be heading back home," James Zook said. "We just wanted to stop by to check on you, and make sure you were doing all right."

Mary wondered if she should tell James and Susan about the sounds she'd heard, but she thought the better of it and said nothing.

"I'm getting familiar with the house," she said. "And I have Fluffy to keep me company." She laughed. "Whoever thought that a cat could keep a person company right inside the house?"

Susan laughed with her. "I know Amish folks keep their cats in the barn."

"Where they belong," Mary added with a grin.

"You can take a break sometime and come over to our home," Susan offered. "Maybe, we can do some Christmas baking together."

"Christmas baking," Mary repeated. And there it was again. The very mention of Christmas reminded her that Lucy was not going to be with them this year – or ever again. And Christmas was the time when she and Lucy did extra baking together.

"My late sister and I used to bake a lot – for the school bake sale especially...and to enjoy with the family," Mary remarked, forcing herself to maintain a pleasant expression.

"Well, the thing to remember, dear, is that you're not alone. You have us – just a call away," Susan said.

"You do have the number I gave you, don't you?" James asked.

Mary looked sheepish. "I'm sorry. I, uh, I seem to have misplaced it."

"Well, I can give it to you again," James said, heaving himself up from the sofa and scrawling his number on the notepad by the telephone.

"We'll be off then," Susan said.

"There's a lot of milk from the cows, and I really can't use all of it," Mary remarked. "The Friesens didn't leave instructions either – of people they possibly supplied."

"They didn't supply anyone," James said.

"I don't mind taking some off you," Susan volunteered. "I could definitely use it in my baking."

"*Gut*," Mary replied, hurrying off to the kitchen to pour some of the milk into jars for Susan to take with her.

Mary's spirits fell as she watched the Zooks drive away, but she went about her chores, determined not to think either of Lucy or of her frightening experiences in the barn and the chicken coop.

But that night, her fears returned as she heard sounds again – the creak of the barn door, a thud, chickens squawking and even the horse whinnying. She lay still in bed, wondering if she should call James, but she couldn't bring herself to, so she tossed through the night, guilty over the fact that someone could even at that moment be stealing something from the barn, and she was allowing it happen by not getting up and going out to investigate.

Chapter Five

Mary began to tremble slightly. She was sitting by the fire with her needlepoint, when she heard a footfall right outside the front door. She glanced at the clock. It was only eight, but still quite late for callers. She tensed, dropping her needle. There was a rapid knocking on the door, and Mary froze; sinking deeper into the couch.

"Mom? Dad?" she heard a deep voice call, and she jumped to her feet and ran to the door. She hesitated only a moment before opening it.

"Uh, hello," Mary said to the young man on the steps, who was staring at her in surprise.

"Who are you?" he asked, running his hand over his chin. From the way he was dressed, he didn't look like he was either Amish or Mennonite, but he had called for his mother and father.

"Who are *you?*" she responded.

"I think you need to tell me where my parents are and what you're doing here." He was craning his neck and trying to see beyond her into the house.

"If your parents are the owners of this house, then you would know where they are, and I wouldn't have to tell you," Mary replied, suddenly nervous that she'd opened the door to a stranger. Yet, he didn't have the appearance of someone dangerous.

The young man sighed. "Look, I'm sorry, but I'm tired. I've traveled all the way from Chicago, and I just want a hot meal and my room to crash in."

"Your room?" Mary asked. Then she blushed. "I'm so sorry. Are you part of the Friesen family?"

"I'm Sam," the young man answered with a nod. "Their son."

"Please...come in," Mary said, stepping aside for Sam to enter.

"Where are Mom and Dad?"

"Didn't they tell you?" Mary asked, puzzled. "They went to Pennsylvania to spend time with a relative who is unwell. I'm here to take care of the house and animals for them."

"I can't imagine why they didn't tell me," Sam declared. "I've been away at university, and I wasn't coming home for the holidays because I got a job. But then I got a few days off and decided to come home for a quick visit." He ran his hand through his hair. "Goodness, but they could have called me. Sorry to alarm you like this, but I assure you, I'm really their son and this really is my home."

"You must be hungry," Mary said briskly, hurrying off into the kitchen. "I'll fix you something to eat."

"Thank you."

It didn't take Mary long to get food on the table. Sam wandered in and observed it laid out nicely for him. "You managed to do all that so quickly?"

Mary blushed. "Well, I had baked the pie earlier today and just heated it up now. And I the stew was a gift from the neighbors—the Zooks." She paused. "Do sit down. I'll make you some hot chocolate as well."

Sam ate hungrily. "This is delicious," he said appreciatively.

"I'm glad you like it," Mary replied, eyeing him covertly and admiring his thick shock of fair hair, grey eyes, and wiry build. She was only slightly aware that Sam was stealing more than a few glances at her simultaneously.

"We need to figure out how to manage this situation," he declared, sipping the cup of hot chocolate Mary handed him.

"*Jah*, we can't both stay here...um...unchaperoned," Mary replied. "So, I'll go home."

"At this hour?" Sam queried. "No way. You can't do that."

"If you would be so kind as to drop me home...or I could request that Mr. Zook come and get me."

Sam shook his head. "No Mary, that wouldn't be fair. You're here at my parents' request to take care of the house—and the animals, too, I imagine—while they're away, and I've arrived unannounced. I'll go and stay with a friend."

"Do you have someone close by?" Mary asked.

"Yes. Nathan Shrock," Sam replied.

"I know the Shrocks," Mary remarked. "They don't live so close by though, do they?"

"With my car, it's not so far." Sam laughed.

"I suppose you're right. Sam?" she asked, on impulse. "You haven't experienced any strange noises around here when you've been home, have you?"

"Strange noises?" Sam queried, wrinkling his nose in a way that Mary found quite endearing.

"Noises in the night," she replied. "The barn door opening and closing. Things in the barn being moved – or used. I counted the apples some days ago and now there are less...and I didn't take any."

"That's odd. And no – we've never experienced anything like that around here," Sam said. "Well, as far as I know. But then,

I haven't been around much lately. I could look into it right now, if you like."

Mary shook her head; although, part of her wanted to encourage him to do just that. Still, he'd just made a long trip and was tired, and he was going to have to find another place to stay.

"*Nee*. It's getting late and you need to get to your friend's house – for which I am already feeling guilty. This is your home and you should rightfully be staying here."

"I'll be around tomorrow. The imagination is a funny thing," he said. "And it can play all sorts of tricks on our minds when we're alone. So, don't worry Mary. There are no ghosts in the barn or wild animals. Sleep well. We'll investigate tomorrow."

"All right. Thank you. *Gut*-night," Mary said as Sam left.

After Sam left, Mary went up to her room, changed, and climbed into bed. After a while, Fluffy jumped up and snuggled down next to her. Funny how quickly she had become accustomed to the cat's presence—in truth, she was enjoying his company.

As she replayed the day's events and dwelt on her encounter with Sam Friesen, she wondered if she was indeed imagining things. Sam had talked about the imagination playing tricks, and she wondered if that could be the case for her. Hadn't her sisters said the very same thing.

But no sooner had the thought crossed her mind, than she heard the sound of the barn door open and close again, and this time, what sounded like footsteps running. She got up and crept to the window to look out, but the winter landscape was dark and the light by the barn wasn't on.

She shook her head in confusion. Had it burnt out? Restless now, she crept downstairs and checked both the front and back doors to make sure they were locked. She was retracing her steps back to her room, when she saw a flash of light outside one of the windows and then heard an accompanying thump. Mary sped up the stairs and closed her bedroom door, huddling under the covers and praying.

"You look tired," Sam remarked, as he strode into the house the next morning.

"I'm afraid I didn't sleep much."

"Bumps in the night again?" Sam quipped.

Mary bit her lip.

"I'm sorry," Sam said. "I didn't mean to poke fun at you. I'm sure your concerns are genuine."

"They are."

"Here," Sam said, scribbling on the pad by the telephone. "That's my cell phone number. Please call me if it happens again, and I will come and take a look. No matter what time of day or night."

"I don't really use the phone," Mary said slowly.

"Mary," Sam said gently. "I know that you aren't permitted the use of modern technology, but in an emergency, you just have to do what you have to do. Please call me if anything happens tonight. Consider that it's part of your job – since you're house sitting, and the safety of the property is your responsibility."

At the sound of the word *responsibility*, Mary looked grave – remembering how she hadn't been able to fulfill her responsibility to Lucy by preventing her from drowning.

"Are you okay?" Sam asked.

"I'm fine," Mary replied, swallowing past the instant lump that had formed in her throat.

"You're very pale."

Mary shook her head. "*Nee.* I'm fine, thank you, Sam."

"Why don't I help with the chores today," he suggested. "You could likely use some help."

"I'm used to heavy work," she declared. "In fact, I quite like it. It helps me forget..." her voice trailed off and she felt her cheeks go hot.

"Forget what?"

"Nothing. I wasn't thinking when I said that," Mary hastily replied.

"You're quite an enigma, aren't you?"

"I lost my sister, Lucy," she blurted and then clapped a hand over her mouth. What in the world was she doing, telling a stranger about Lucy? This wasn't like her at all.

"Oh... I'm so sorry," Sam replied. "You can tell me about it if you want to."

Something about the kindness in his voice drew Mary. Without thinking, she sat down heavily on the sofa and sighed.

"It was summer, and we were down by the river. Lucy wanted to get in the water, and I reminded her that we were not permitted to. The river is deep, though it appears deceptively shallow. I was busy picking wild blackberries when I heard a scream. Lucy had jumped in and was unable to swim. I'm sure she imagined she could paddle about, but of course, she couldn't. I jumped in and tried to save her myself, but I couldn't get to her. I tried. *Ach,* how I tried. The current carried her away..."

Sam was silent for a long minute, and then he murmured, "Oh Mary, I had no idea. I'm really sorry."

Tears spilled down Mary's cheeks. "I couldn't save my own sister. And she was my responsibility."

"But it wasn't your fault, Mary. You tried to save her."

"But I couldn't," Mary replied. "My family was kind to me through the whole ordeal. B-but I should have saved her. Or stopped her from going in."

"You can't feel responsible for Lucy's death, Mary, because it wasn't your fault," Sam said gently.

"Everybody keeps telling me that," Mary replied miserably, "but I still feel weighed down. I can't forget her. I can't forget the sight of her body...lying so still and cold."

"I'm so sorry."

"Look, I-I should get on with my chores," Mary said, getting to her feet and sweeping her tears away with the back of her hand.

"I'm going to help you today...whether you like it or not," Sam declared. "What should we do first?"

"I've already milked the cows," Mary said. "But I haven't seen to Roasted Chestnut or the chickens."

"Roasted Chestnut?" Sam laughed. "That's a charming name. Are you talking about our horse?"

Mary turned pink. "Oh, I just call him that because I don't know his real name."

Sam shrugged. "Dad calls him Tinder," he said. "But in truth, I like Roasted Chestnut much better. RC for short."

Mary laughed. "All right. At least, while I'm here."

After bundling up, they went outside together. Mary glanced around, wondering whether she'd see any evidence of an intruder. She saw nothing.

"I'll get some grain," Mary said, hurrying to the barn and stopping short as she put out a hand to open the door.

"Sam," she said, her voice trembling.

"What is it?" Sam asked.

"There's...b-blood...on the door." She stared at the red smears with her heart pounding in her chest. Was someone hurt? She froze. Was one of the animals hurt?

Sam ran to Mary's side, and the two of them stared at the red on the barn door.

"I think we need to call the police," he whispered. "This looks serious."

"Will you call them?" Mary asked. "I-I'd feel better staying here if I knew the police had checked the place thoroughly for signs of intruders."

Chapter Six

The police didn't take long to arrive. Mary stammered out answers to their questions.

"So, you're Mary Lapp," one of the policemen said, after she gave him her name. "I'm Officer Wilson, and this is my colleague Officer Martin. Are you possibly a relative of Lucy Lapp...the girl who...?"

"Drowned?" Mary asked. "*Jah*, I'm her older sister."

Somehow the past was always going to haunt her, one way or the other. "How do you know about her?"

"I work both Cedarwood and Dovetail Villages. I remember when it happened," the policeman replied. "I recall my colleague reporting that the girl with her, her older sister, was severely traumatized by the incident."

"Yes, and that's over and done with, Officer Wilson," Sam said politely but firmly. "Now, we're dealing with the possibility of an intruder on our premises."

"Mr. Friesen," Officer Wilson said, "were you present when Mary heard the odd sounds?"

"No, I was not," he replied. "But right now, we're more concerned about the blood on the door."

"We don't know whose it is now, do we?" Officer Wilson countered. "You mentioned that you came by this morning – and that Mary led you to the barn."

"I didn't lead Sam to the barn at all. I was going to fetch grain to feed the horse," Mary said.

Officer Wilson turned to Sam again. "Is it possible that you cut yourself without knowing it? That perhaps the blood is yours?" He must have seen the expression on her face, for he quickly continued, "We have to explore every possibility."

"I assure you that I didn't do that," Mary said, now wishing that the police hadn't been called at all. "Take a look at my hands and you will see there's no wound that would cause the blood that's on the barn door."

"We'll take a careful look around," Officer Wilson said. "That's about all we can do. If we see something suspicious, we can follow up. Other than that..."

"We understand," Sam said. "And we do appreciate you taking a look around."

The police found nothing out of the ordinary. Mary stood by, watching them, uneasiness filling her stomach. She'd gotten the distinct impression that the police thought she was fabricating things, and she hoped she was wrong.

As the police drove away, Mary looked at Sam. "Officer Wilson thinks I've lost my mind and am imagining things, doesn't he?"

"Like he said, he has to check on every possibility, that's all," Sam replied. "Please don't feel badly about this, Mary. We'll get to the bottom of things one way or the other."

"I don't blame Officer Wilson," Mary said later, as she and Sam sat down at the table with cups of tea and biscuits. "I was such a mess after Lucy's death. I couldn't stop crying. I couldn't eat, sleep, or think straight, and I couldn't stand to be in company. Perhaps I am crazy after all."

Sam set down his cup and looked into Mary's clear blue eyes.

"You're not crazy, Mary," he said. "The way you reacted to the trauma of losing your beloved sister was natural. It was understandably a huge shock to your system. I admire that you conduct yourself with such grace after going through it all."

Mary searched his eyes. No one had ever said that to her before. Did he really admire her for getting through it? She smiled, feeling a warmth in her heart that seemed almost strange in its unlikeliness. "Thank you for saying that, Sam," she murmured, meaning it with her whole heart.

As she watched Sam drive away later that day, Mary felt her spirits plummet again. She wished there was some way she could have someone stay in the house with her. As if in answer to her wish, there was a knock on the front door not an hour later.

"Becky! Sarah!" Mary exclaimed.

"*Ach,* Mary. We've missed you," they chorused, coming into the house.

"But we have to rush," Becky said. "*Mamm* has us busy baking for the school's Christmas program..."

"And since I'm helping with the program," Sarah said, "I have to get the children ready for the Nativity Play."

"You both sound happy and busy."

"We are – because it's all to do with Christmas," Sarah replied. "And how are you?"

"I have my hands full, too," Mary answered. "Doing all the chores by myself is quite a task, but I've had company."

"Really? Who?" Becky asked.

"Fluffy," Mary replied, picking up the cat who had just strolled in, and introducing him to her sisters. She didn't know why, but she couldn't bring herself to tell them anything about Sam.

"You look a bit tired," Becky remarked.

"I'm actually tired of hearing people say I'm tired," Mary said, hearing the edge to her voice. She laughed, trying to cover her tone.

"We've been making Christmas gifts, too," Sarah said.

"You have?" Mary queried, feeling a stab of guilt that she hadn't even begun to think about gifts, and Christmas was just two weeks away.

"*Jah*," Sarah replied, and animatedly began to describe all that they had been making.

Mary listened with a fixed smile on her face; her thoughts wandering off to dwell on Sam instead. She wondered what he was doing right then and whether he would come back to visit her later.

"Mary...Mary?" Becky said, peering into her face anxiously. "You're a million miles away."

Mary chuckled. "Perhaps I nodded off with my eyes wide open."

"Nobody does that, Mary. *Ach*, we'd better get back home," Becky said. "Come on, Sarah."

"*Mamm* sent you some food. I left it in the buggy by mistake," Sarah said.

"I'll come outside with you both and get it," Mary replied, flashing her sisters a bright smile. "I could do with some of *Mamm's* special cooking. Do tell her that I am enjoying all the preserves she insisted I bring with me."

Mary walked out to the buggy with her sisters, and Sarah climbed in to get the basket of food.

"Hurry up, Sarah," Becky said impatiently, when Sarah took longer than expected. "Why are you looking under the seats for the basket of food?"

"Because it must have slipped off the seat and I didn't realize it," Sarah said, sounding mystified.

"Goodness sake, I'll help you look for it," Becky offered, climbing in the other side of the buggy and leaning down, practically on her hands and knees.

"It's not here. This is really odd. I'm sure I saw Sarah carry the basket to the buggy and set it on the seat. Or maybe we were so preoccupied with all that we've been doing that we thought we'd carried it to the buggy and actually didn't," Becky suggested, sounding perturbed.

Mary stiffened. "You'll know when you get back home whether you actually brought the basket or not," she said quietly, trying to still the rapid beating of her heart. "You didn't happen to notice anyone in the yard when you arrived, did you?"

"*Nee*, I didn't," Sarah replied.

"Neither did I," Becky added.

After Sarah and Becky had driven away, Mary looked for footprints, but all she saw was a mix of prints that could have been anyone's. While she was peering at the earth, she again experienced the sensation of being observed. She jerked upright and hurried to the barn. Once inside, she counted the apples, and found that they had further decreased in number, though she hadn't taken any after the first pie she had baked.

She found an empty gunnysack and filled it with the rest of the apples, leaving only one in the crate, and carried the sack into the house. Then she went to the chicken coop to look for any freshly laid eggs and collected those in a basket.

"I wish the Friesens believed in locks," Mary murmured to herself as she went back indoors and searched for something with which to secure the chicken coop. Finally, she gave up, and decided to make a trip to Dovetail Market. This time, however, she locked the front door and took the key with her.

Chapter Seven

"Mary Lapp, *ain't so?*" the jolly lady at the Dovetail Market greeted her.

Mary smiled and nodded. "I need to buy some pretty paper to make Christmas greetings."

"Over here. Take a look," the lady said, showing her a display against the wall.

Mary gazed at the beautiful array and chose three different styles. The saleslady slipped the paper Mary had chosen into a bag, took her money, and handed the bag to her. "You're that Amish gal staying over at the Friesen's farm while they're away, I hear," she remarked.

"*Jah*," Mary answered, nodding.

"Heard you had to call the police because you found blood on the barn door," the lady continued.

Mary flushed. "News travels fast," she murmured. Though it was the same in her district, to be sure. "Umm, is there any history of thefts in Dovetail Village?"

"Not usually, dear. This city is as safe as Cedarwood. Not much crime at all. Ask anyone..." The lady's brow furrowed and she leaned forward as if ready to reveal a huge secret. "You should just rest, dear, and maybe join in some of the Christmas activities...to get your mind off... Well, you know."

"I take it Officer Wilson told you my sister drowned in an accident?"

"This is a small town," the lady replied. "And we're all like family. Believe me, we're all concerned about you."

"I'm fine," Mary said crisply. "I did suffer a lot of heartache over losing my dear sister, but that doesn't mean I'm imagining things."

"Of course, it doesn't," the lady said, clucking her tongue. "I completely understand."

Mary stood still, goosebumps on her arms, the sensation of being watched now even more intense.

"What's wrong?" the lady queried. "You're white as a sheet."

"Nothing's wrong," Mary replied, mustering a smile. "I suppose I just remembered how many things I need to do... and how close Christmas is."

She left the store quickly, jumped on her bicycle, and pedaled furiously back to the Friesen's farm. She didn't like being the subject of people's wagging tongues.

The daylight began to fade as Mary rode along, and she had to stop to switch on the battery light on the bicycle. She felt shivers snake down her spine and scolded herself for being so afraid when Dovetail Village was obviously a safe place. Hadn't the saleslady just assured her of that very fact?

Nevertheless, Mary heaved a huge sigh of relief when she made it safely back to the Friesen's house. She lit a fire in the grate and made herself a cup of hot tea. She had bought Fluffy some fish, and she put it out on a plate on the steps leading down from the kitchen, because she couldn't see the cat anywhere.

She put on her shawl and hustled outside to the chicken coop, avoiding even glancing at the barn, and quickly checked on the poultry before running back to the house. As she ran up the steps, her eyes fell on the plate just inside the door where, not even a quarter of an hour earlier, she had placed the fish for Fluffy to come and eat. The plate lay there – licked clean, with not even a scale or the tail left.

Mary picked up the plate and then searched every room – afraid now because she had left the kitchen door ajar when she had gone to check on the chickens. Had Fluffy gotten out?

"Fluffy!" she called. "Fluffy?"

But there was no answering meow, no rubbing of a soft furry body against her legs. Mary searched the entire house and finally flopped down on the sofa, exhausted and not a little worried.

The telephone rang and, as always, Mary jumped. Before she could answer, the voice machine kicked on.

"Hello Mary," Mrs. Friesen's voice echoed in the silence. "Sam called to say he had come home to give us a surprise and met you. He told me you were coping well with all the chores and had made friends with Fluffy. If you need anything, I suppose it will be simpler to call Sam as he's staying close enough at the Shrocks. I did ask him if he'd take over the house sitting, so that you could return to your home earlier, but he said he had to get back to his campus job. Well, you take care then. Let me know if you need anything. Bye."

Mary heard a thud in her bedroom and froze. But in a flash, she realized it had to be Fluffy moving about, and she relaxed. When he wandered into the front room, she picked him up. Funny, but she didn't smell a bit of fish on his breath. Usually after eating the treat, he smelled so strongly, it was almost offensive. But this time, nothing.

Had Fluffy even eaten the fish? She lay back against the sofa and mentally replayed her sisters' visit when an entire basket of food was presumably missing from their buggy.

Chapter Eight

That night, Mary woke up to the sound of agitated clucking from the chicken coop. The poultry were clearly in distress. Mary imagined herself brave enough to confront her fears and go outside to investigate, but instead, she pulled the covers over her head and prayed. When the sounds died down, she contemplated going downstairs and phoning Sam, but dismissed the idea almost as soon as it came to her. She couldn't be bothering him in the middle of the night, no matter what he'd said.

At dawn, she was still too afraid to go outside, so she washed, dressed and began to clean the house. Later that morning, she stood before the telephone and stared at the two numbers on the writing pad. One was James Zook's number and the other was Sam's. Should she call one of them?

At length, she picked up the telephone receiver and held it to her ear, listening to the dial tone; her fingers poised to press the numbers. When she heard the gravel crunch in the driveway, Mary's first emotion was one of relief that someone was coming to the house. Her second was also relief – that she didn't have to call anyone.

"Sam," she exclaimed when she opened the door. "Am I relieved to see you."

"Another sleepless night, I can tell," Sam remarked worriedly. "What happened?"

"The chickens were going crazy...so much so that I even contemplated going out in the middle of the night to investigate."

"I'm glad you decided not to," Sam said. "Who knows what you may have encountered. I know everyone likes to think that Dovetail Village is the safest place on earth, but we need to realize that things can and do happen everywhere."

"Could you come with me please to check on the chickens?" she asked. "I honestly haven't had the courage to go out just yet...and I was at the point of phoning you when you arrived."

"Of course, I'll come with you," Sam replied. With a half-smile, he added, "You were going to call me, huh? Well, good for you."

They went outside and as they passed the barn door, Mary stopped and pointed at it. It wasn't tightly shut.

"I closed it – I know I did," she said.

"We'll get back there and take a look," Sam said. "Let's check the chicken coop first."

"Oh my," Mary gasped, as she looked inside the coop and saw what had to be the remnants of a chicken. Loose feathers were scattered across the frozen ground. She rapidly counted all the rest and found that another hen was missing.

"Look here," Sam said, pointing to a gap where the fence appeared to have been ripped open. "I'm not sure what...or who...could have done that."

"A fox, perhaps," Mary said, still staring at the remains of the hapless bird whose body had been torn into quite violently.

"It could be," Sam replied. "But you know, we've lived here so long, and this has never happened. Not once. The fence is strong."

"Should we check the barn now?" Mary asked, unable to keep a tremor from her voice.

"Absolutely. And Mary, don't be afraid. We'll face it together," Sam reassured her; taking her hand in his as they neared the barn.

"More apples were missing from the crates, so I took the rest of them indoors."

"That was smart," Sam replied.

Sam pushed the door fully open, and she gasped.

"There are apples in one of the crates," she said. "How is that possible when I only left one behind?"

"Maybe you left more than one there, without realizing it," Sam suggested.

"*Nee* Sam, I'm absolutely sure that I didn't." Mary said vehemently. "Is someone trying to make me look crazy?" As soon as the words were out of her mouth, she felt ridiculous.

"Who would do that Mary? And why?" Sam asked.

Mary shook her head. "All I know is that I emptied all the crates and now there's one with apples in it."

"Look," Sam said. "Why don't I take you out to do something that will take your mind off all of this? Maybe we could go out for supper in town?"

"*Nee.* I'm here to take care of your parents' home, and I should focus on that. I've already lost another hen."

"And I think you could do with a change, so I say yes," Sam urged.

"All right," Mary agreed, albeit grudgingly. "I guess we could have an early supper."

"And I'm going to spend the morning fixing the fence."

"I'll help you," Mary said. "I'm not too bad at fixing fences."

"Well, let's get down to it then," Sam replied, reaching for a tool kit that lay on one of the shelves in the barn.

Back at the coop, Sam hunkered down to examine the damage more closely. He frowned and shook his head. "You know, this looks like it's been torn open by some kind of implement, rather than by an animal."

Mary crouched down beside Sam and looked at the hole. She had shoved up the side flaps of her cape, and as her sleeve brushed against Sam's, she felt something zap between them, and for a brief instant Sam turned and their eyes met.

"You're right," Mary said, standing up quickly and smoothing down her cape. "It couldn't have been done by an animal."

"There was the one chicken that had been mauled...and the other was missing with no trace of any remains, so it's possible that one chicken was stolen by a human being and the other by an animal. But I'm just speculating," Sam said.

"I guess I should go inside and get on with the rest of my chores," Mary murmured.

Sam reached up and took her hand, pulling her gently down beside him. "Stay and help me, Mary."

She sighed and knelt down beside him. She shouldn't stay out here. It was cold and she was upset and... She closed her eyes for a brief moment. The truth of it was, she shouldn't be out here with Sam because she was beginning to feel things for him. Things that she shouldn't. He was Mennonite. She was Amish.

And they were too close together.

"Would you hold the wire down while I clip it in place and then hammer in some nails?" Sam asked.

"*Jah*," Mary replied, feeling a little warm and breathless. She stole a glance at Sam from the corner of her eye and then looked down at his hands – large and strong - as they expertly mended the fence. Sam didn't need her help at all, but for some reason, he'd wanted her company.

"You're very brave, you know," Sam remarked.

"What makes you say that?"

"Well, just the fact that you didn't go running back home despite the very real fear of an intruder here," Sam replied.

"If I were truly brave, I would have come running out last night and chased away the intruder – human or animal...but I chose not to."

"And just so you know – I don't think you're imagining anything."

"Not even the whole mystery of the apples which appear to have come back by themselves?" Mary asked with a wry laugh.

"If you say you emptied the crates of all the apples, but one, then you did," Sam declared. "Besides, you'll have the sack of apples inside to prove it."

"You're a nice person."

"So are you, Mary," Sam replied. He stood and went back to the barn to put the tool kit on the shelf. He came back out and closed the door behind him.

Mary was waiting for him and together, they walked back toward the house.

"Tell me more about your life in Cedarwood," Sam said, falling into step with her.

"There's nothing much to tell," Mary replied. "Cedarwood Village is much like any Amish district I suppose, where everyone knows everyone else...and where nothing can happen without everybody knowing when, where, and how it happened."

Sam laughed. "That sounds very much like Dovetail," he replied. "There's nothing that can happen here without the whole of the town from our farm to Dovetail Market and beyond...knowing everything in the minutest detail."

Mary looked at him. "What is it like...being a Mennonite?"

Sam chuckled. "I imagine not unlike being Amish," he replied. "Except that we are not as strict." He shrugged. "I choose to dress like an *Englischer* because I go to University and want to fit in. I do, however, tell everyone I'm a Mennonite, and that I have certain rules I adhere to."

"Like?" Mary asked.

"Like...well...dating, for instance. I take it seriously. So, I have never dated casually."

She bit the inside of her lip. She felt a bit uncomfortable speaking about such things.

"See, we might have electricity, a telephone, and cars, but we still live a fairly simple life."

"I see."

"Especially on our farm," Sam replied. "Dad only recently has begun using a tractor. Until then, we used an old-fashioned plough. And we still avoid the use of chemicals in the fields."

He gave her a keen look and smiled. "So...not so different then, are we?"

Mary smiled. "I suppose not."

"Plus, I love Shoofly Pie." Sam laughed.

Mary burst into laughter along with him. "Then I shall make you one."

"I was hoping you'd say that." He looked away and then back at her; his gaze intense. "Mary, I have to get back to the Shrocks', but I'll be back to pick you up at five o'clock. Will that be all right with you?"

She nodded. "*Jah*."

"Not too nervous about being on your own, are you?"

"*Nee*," she replied. "I have Christmas decorations and greetings to make and chores to finish, and a mystery to mull over."

He smiled. "I'll see you at five then."

After he left, Mary sat out on the front step for a while, until the chilly breeze drove her inside once again.

She sat at the dining table and took out the paints and brushes she had bought at the market and started on her Christmas greetings. She paused midway in the activity as it suddenly struck her that she hadn't been thinking of Lucy as much as before. It seemed as if Sam was taking over her thoughts lately – his smile, his laugh, his hands; and just the way he was – gentle and kind.

Mary took her favorite dark blue dress out of the closet and smoothed it down; hoping that Sam wouldn't find her too plain in it. She put it on and then rewound her hair into a bun. She pinned her *kapp* firmly in place and looked into the mirror hanging over the dresser. Her cheeks were flushed, and her eyes gleamed.

There was no way to deny it—she was excited. A whole

evening with Sam. The very thought of it sent her heart racing.

The sound of his car in the drive sent her scurrying to the front door. Was he early? She threw it open as James Zook got out of his car. Her heart plummeted in disappointment, but she worked to hide it from this kind neighbor.

"Mr. Zook," Mary greeted him warmly. "How are you today?"

"How are you?" James asked. "I heard about the ruined fence in the chicken coop and came over to check on you."

"But who told you about it?" Mary asked.

"I met Sam at the Shrocks' home," James Zook explained. "And he told me."

"It's so kind of you to come over."

"It's the least I can do," James replied. "Sam told me that he fixed it, but I wish you weren't out here all by yourself."

Mary shrugged. "It's not for much longer."

"Yes. I suggested to the Friesens that I send one of my farmhands over to take care of their animals while you're away for Christmas."

"But aren't the Friesens going to be back by Christmas?"

James Zook shook his head. "Apparently not."

"And Sam? Where will he be?"

"Back on campus, I should think," James Zook replied. "Which is why I volunteered to send someone down to take care of things at the house here."

"I see," Mary said. She looked toward the gate and saw a buggy turning into the drive. It was Sarah and Becky.

"Who is that?" James Zook asked, turning to stare at the buggy that was rumbling towards them.

"My sisters."

"They seem excited...or agitated," he observed.

"Mary!" Sarah said, without preamble, as she jumped out of the buggy. "We didn't forget the basket the other day. We did bring it...so—"

"It was stolen," Becky chimed in, joining her on the drive. "Which means there's someone or something here that..."

"Sarah, Becky, this is Mr. James Zook. Mr. Zook, these are my sisters – come all the way from Cedarwood to visit me," Mary said.

"What is this about a stolen basket?" James asked. "That is mighty curious. Things like that don't happen here in Dovetail."

"I'm sure there's some other explanation for what happened," Mary murmured, wanting to make light of it, now. She was becoming weary of this intruder business. It was taking over her entire life. "Will you all come in?"

"We just brought you another basket of goodies," Sarah said, ducking back into the buggy and presenting Mary with a brimming basket.

"And *Mamm* said to tell you that *Daed* will come and fetch you day after tomorrow so that you can come home for an afternoon of Christmas baking with us. They felt you might be missing out on all the holiday activities."

"Thank *Mamm* for the food," Mary replied. "And I'll be ready for *Daed* to fetch me."

"You are coming home for Christmas, aren't you, Mary?" Sarah asked.

"*Jah*...of course...if someone will fetch me on Christmas Eve."

"We can't come in, but we'll see you soon, all right?" Sarah said.

"All right. See you soon."

Chapter Nine

"It must be hard living here on your own," James remarked, as Mary waved goodbye to her sisters.

"*Nee*. It's fine," she said, suddenly wishing that everyone would stop worrying about her.

"The Friesens will be grateful to you for taking care of their animals for them."

"Thank you for checking up on me, Mr. Zook," Mary said. "Really, it's most kind."

"The people of Dovetail are a very close-knit community," he said. "And we also tend to be protective about our people."

"I see."

"So if at times, it might seem that nobody believes what you are saying about noises in the night or thefts, it's only because nobody wants to acknowledge that things like this may actually happen here. If you know what I mean."

"I appreciate your concern."

James sighed heavily. "Mary, the thing is, we have experienced something similar to what you have described – noises at night, things going missing, and a sense of not quite being alone."

Mary exhaled sharply. "What? And you've never told anyone? I don't understand."

James gave her a contrite look. "I'm sorry. We thought it was nothing. You can understand that, surely. My apologies for not admitting this to you before."

Mary didn't know what to say. At least, she wasn't going crazy.

"We're a peace-loving community," he continued. "And whoever was causing the disturbance couldn't possibly be one of us, so we saw no need to make too much of what was going on."

"Maybe," Mary replied wanting nothing more at that point to either go home or be left alone. "You have been very kind, and so has Sam Friesen...and the people at the market."

"Please lock your doors at night and by day as well," James Zook said.

"Has Officer Wilson found out anything, or do you know?"

"He took up the matter immediately after coming at your behest the other day. But of course, I have no idea what he actually has been able to do."

After James left, Mary carried the basket form her mother inside and put the food into the refrigerator. She looked out of the kitchen window, determined not to draw the curtains. She saw the barn door swing open of its own accord.

She hurried to check that the house doors were bolted from the inside, and even checked the windows – and then returned to her position by the kitchen window. She sat there for a very long time but saw no movement at all...until the chickens began to squawk in apparent distress.

Mary got to her feet, picked up the broom and ran to the chicken coop, only to find that it was open and two chickens already outside. She hurriedly returned them to the coop and shut the door, then went indoors again, and sank into a sofa, gasping for breath.

When the hour drew near for Sam to pick her up for supper in town, Mary waited eagerly by the door. He was on time, and Mary went out to meet him, turning around to lock the front door, looking furtively around her as she did so.

"You seem a little on edge," Sam remarked, as Mary slid the key into her bag.

"I can tell you all about it on the way," she replied. "And I think you're right – a change will do me good."

"What happened?" Sam asked. "You are really quite pale."

Mary sighed. "I don't mean to lay my troubles on you, or to be a discouraging companion. It's just that there was another incident today – and the chicken coop was left open. Fortunately, I reached it in time to get the two chickens who had run out, back inside, and I secured the coop as best as I could."

"Are you certain you didn't leave the coop open unintentionally? Maybe you were distracted with something when you were leaving after feeding the chickens, and you didn't realize that you didn't close the door?"

Mary shook her head in exasperation. "You're beginning to think like certain others, Sam. *Nee,* I didn't leave the coop open. I was indoors and the chickens started squawking in a frenzy...so I ran out to check on them and found the coop open."

"Let's not quarrel," Sam said softly, driving with one hand and laying his other hand on Mary's.

Mary slid her hand out from under Sam's and sat stiff and upright in her seat.

"It's not that I don't believe what you told me just now," Sam said. "Of course, I do. I just had to be sure, that's all."

"*Jah,* that's what everyone keeps saying, isn't it? Be sure, because this is Mary Lapp we're talking about – the girl who lost her mind because her sister drowned while under her care."

"Nobody says that, Mary. Truly, they don't. Please don't use that as an excuse to shut people out."

Mary glared at him. "I don't know what you're talking about."

"I think you do. If you actually believed people genuinely cared about the girl who lost her sister, then you'd be compelled to let people into your life, but this way – this way you don't have to, do you?"

"If we weren't halfway to town, I'd ask you to take me back to the farm," she replied, thoroughly annoyed now.

"You don't have to do anything that you don't want to," Sam said. "But right now, I'd very much like us to enjoy the supper we planned. I have to get back to campus early tomorrow morning."

"Oh," Mary murmured, her chest tightening. She took a deep, slow breath. What was the matter with her? Sam was only trying to help. She didn't have to get all upset. "I'm sorry. I don't want you to go away thinking I'm a horrid person... because you've really helped me through the past few days and..."

"No. I'm sorry. I should have kept my big mouth shut. Let's just enjoy our evening, shall we?"

"The shops look so beautiful, all lit up," Mary exclaimed in delight, her spirits lifting. There were Christmas lights strung everywhere, twinkling in the darkness.

"That's why I wanted to bring you here. I felt like you could do with some Christmas cheer," Sam said.

As they walked through the decorated streets, with the cheerful shops on either side, Sam gazed down at Mary – her face was completely transformed and joyful as she took in all the sights.

"There are so many people out and about, even though it's cold," Mary remarked with a shiver. She grasped her woolen cape more securely around herself. "Do you think it will snow tonight?"

"It might. I wouldn't be surprised. I called ahead and made a booking at a restaurant I think you'll love," Sam said. "I was lucky to get us a table, though, as it's always full."

"Oh my," Mary exclaimed as they walked into the quaint old restaurant Sam had chosen for them. It was called Diner's Delight, and it was festooned with lights, decorations, a Christmas tree, and even what appeared to be snowflakes drifting around the tables.

"How did they do that?" Mary asked, trying to catch the snowflakes in her hand.

"It's all a trick of lighting," Sam explained.

"It's incredible," Mary said, her eyes shining.

Sam took Mary's arm as they followed a waitress, dressed as a Christmas Elf, to their table. He pulled out her chair for her and seated her, before he sat down opposite and gazed into her eyes.

"You look quite happy," he remarked, clearly pleased with himself.

"I am," Mary answered. "I've never been out like this ever before in all my eighteen years. It's ... why, it's magical."

"To be honest, I've never been out like this in all my twenty-two years," Sam declared, almost shyly.

"Really? How did you know about this place?"

"I've walked past it every Christmas since I turned sixteen," Sam said. "And I vowed I would come for supper here with the first girl I ever thought of courting."

Mary's eyes widened in disbelief. "S-Sam," she stammered. "What are you saying?"

"I'd like to formally court you, Mary," Sam replied, reaching across the table to lay his hand over hers.

"B-but..."

"Why does that surprise you?" Sam laughed. "You must have known, from the first moment we met, that I was drawn to you."

She gently pulled her hand from his and clasped her hands tightly in her lap. Her heart thudded against her ribs. Could this be true? She liked him—liked him so much, but—

"So Mary...will you let me court you?"

"I would, Sam," Mary whispered, "but I'm Amish..."

"And I'm Mennonite." Sam laughed. "And except for the few modern conveniences we've incorporated into our lifestyle, we aren't that different." Sam cleared his throat. "Besides, I think... Well, I think I'm falling in love with you."

Mary's mouth dropped open. "Sam..."

Before she could say another word, Sam held up his hand. "No. Don't say anything more, Mary. Let me finish saying what I have to say. I haven't been able to stay away from seeing you every day since we met. And I can only say that it was the Good Lord above who brought us together. Can you honestly think of any other reason why you would be staying at the farm...and why I was suddenly free to visit my parents, not knowing they had gone to Pennsylvania?"

Mary looked into Sam's eyes.

"Are you ready to order?" the waitress with the elf costume interrupted them.

"Yes. Yes, thank you," Sam replied.

"I'm not very hungry all of a sudden," Mary said, staring at the menu with unseeing eyes.

"Should I go ahead and order two holiday specials?" Sam asked.

"It sounds like a lot of food." Mary laughed.

"It's Christmas on a plate," the waitress explained, adjusting her elf hat.

"Something we both need," Sam said.

The waitress scurried off, and Sam took Mary's hand again. He didn't say anymore, but his eyes rested on hers. Around them, the restaurant buzzed with activity. People were chatting and laughing, and the air was full of festivity.

Mary's mind went to Lucy. She saw again her sister's wide eyes of wonder whenever they went for a walk down by the river. She heard again her sister's joyous giggle when she said something silly. She remembered Lucy's excitement about Christmas and all the wonderful company and food.

Lucy would never again enjoy the holidays. And Mary would never again enjoy Lucy. Was it all right then? Was it all right for Mary to enjoy Christmas without her precious sister?

Just then, she heard a young girl laugh at the next table. Mary looked over at her and felt a sense of peace settle in her heart. Yes. It was all right. She could enjoy Christmas. She *could*.

Not too many minutes later, the waitress brought their meals.

"I don't think I can eat all of this," Mary said, looking down at her plate. But she dug into it with gusto, and later Sam laughed as he remarked about how clean her plate was.

"It was delicious," Mary said. "I haven't ever had such a delightful meal."

"This restaurant expands for the holidays. They rent additional space during November and December only," Sam said. "So, it's really special that I'm here with you."

Mary smiled into Sam's eyes but said nothing. She was already dreading the next day when he would return to his university. As if reading her thoughts, he said, "I'll be back before you know it, Mary, and I hope you'll have an answer for me."

"Do you have to go?"

"A job on campus is a big deal, so yes, I do have to go, but I'll be back on Christmas Day," he replied. "At which point, I'd like to meet your parents and ask their permission to court you...if you say yes., that is."

Chapter Ten

Mary lay awake for a long time, replaying the events of the day and lingering long on her memories of dinner with Sam. He had been attentive and caring, but most of all, he had asked to court her. She had never met anyone like Sam before, nor had she harbored feelings for any man before him. But he was a Mennonite, and therefore her parents might not be in favor of the union.

Mary's eyes misted over, missing Sam already, and wondered why life was so ironic as to bring someone like him into her life and then make it next to impossible for them to be together. People might think of the Amish and Mennonites as the same, or two sides of the same coin, but would her parents feel the same way? She knew her father had good friends who were Mennonites, but that didn't mean he'd want one courting her.

She fell into a restless sleep and woke to the sound of the barn door slamming. She froze in her bed and pulled her covers over her head. She began to panic when the barn door creaked open and shut repeatedly, and even the cows began to low.

Leaving the warmth and comfort of her bed, Mary inched toward her bedroom door and down the stairs. This time, she was determined to pick up the telephone and call Sam. She couldn't take the fear and anxiety anymore.

She dialed the number and waited with a pounding heart for Sam to answer.

"It's happening again," Mary whispered breathlessly into the phone, "and this time I am terrified because all the animals are disturbed."

"I'll be right there," Sam said. "Stay indoors and don't go outside for anything."

Mary called James Zook next. There was safety in numbers, she said to herself.

"I'm on my way, and I'll call Officer Wilson, too," James Zook told her.

Mary lowered the wick of her oil lamp and sat in the semi darkness; her heart pounding in fear as she heard the sound of footsteps outside the kitchen door.

She called Sam again. "I'm sorry Sam, but I am out of my mind with fear."

"Don't worry, Mary, I'm on my way, and I'm bringing Nathan and his dad as well. When we arrive, don't come out. Stay inside while we deal with whatever it is that's causing the disturbance," Sam instructed her. "We're going to leave the car outside the gate and come in on foot so that we don't give the intruder the chance to hear us.

Mary peeped furtively out of the window at regular intervals, but she couldn't see anything in the darkness. All at once, she heard the roar of a car engine, followed by the thump of running feet, and clapped her hand over her mouth. She had never been so afraid in her life. She didn't want to be alone in the house where she could be cornered, so, emboldened by the imminent arrival of her friends, Mary slid out of the front door and crept toward the gate, keeping to the shadows.

"Mary!" a hoarse whisper stopped her in her tracks.

"Sam?"

"What are you doing outside? I told you to stay inside. It's far too dangerous."

"I don't want to be alone inside," Mary whispered. "I'm coming along with you, no matter what."

"I'm waiting for a signal from Officer Wilson," Sam said, crouching by the edge of the barn. "Officer Wilson and Mr. Zook have gone in ahead of me."

"I hope they get to the bottom of this nightmare."

Just then, a figure ran toward them – not seeing them in the gloom - and almost collided with Mary. Sam turned around swiftly and went after the person, still not discernible in the darkness. Mary picked up her skirts and sprinted after Sam.

"Get back!" they heard Officer Wilson cry. "Stop and don't move!"

Their ears were filled once again by the sound of running feet, and Mary stopped abruptly, her eyes sweeping the periphery for signs of whoever it was.

A shadowy figure came running full tilt and almost collided with her once again. Mary stuck out her leg, and the person tripped and fell, letting out a loud howl as he did so.

The next few minutes were a blur, as Sam threw himself at the person on the ground and held him fast as Mary cried out for James Zook and Officer Wilson, who joined them almost immediately.

Officer Wilson turned a flashlight onto the person Sam had pinned down, and everyone gasped. It was a young boy.

"What on earth are you doing here, boy?" Sam asked indignantly.

The boy said nothing. He couldn't have been more than fourteen or fifteen years old, and he appeared petrified at the sight of Sam, Officer Wilson, James Zook, Nathan and his father, and Mary.

"What do you want with me?" the boy asked, his voice surly.

"The question you need to answer is, what are you doing here? How long have you been skulking around the premises?" Officer Wilson countered.

The boy remained mutinously silent until Mary spoke up.

"Was it you who stole a chicken from the coop, a fish from the kitchen, and apples from the barn?" she asked.

"I don't have to answer to you," he snarled. "You don't own this house."

"Watch your tongue," Sam ordered. "Answer the lady's question."

"I need to eat, don't I?" the boy spat out bitterly.

"Where do you stay?" Officer Wilson asked.

The boy made an attempt to spring out of Sam's grip and bolt, but Sam held him fast.

"Go on," Officer Wilson prodded. "Tell us where you live."

"I don't live no place," the boy blurted, "and that barn there was empty." He turned to Mary. "I put the apples back," he said defensively, "and I would have returned the fish and the chicken as well except I don't got 'em no more."

"You shouldn't have stolen anything in the first place," Sam said firmly.

"Who are your parents?" Officer Wilson asked. "I need to contact them."

The boy shook his head. "Please...Officer...don't call my parents," he pleaded. "I will tell you everything you need to know...and I'll work and earn enough to return all that food I stole."

"You stole my basket of food as well, I suppose?" Mary asked. "And was it your blood on the barn door?"

"Can't you dumb people understand?" the boy cried. "I was hungry. And I got hurt when I tried to get into the chicken coop."

"Even so, that doesn't justify theft," Officer Wilson replied.

"So was it your blood on the barn door?" Sam echoed Mary's query. "Do you need medical attention?"

"How long have you been in the barn?" Mary asked.

"From before you got here," the boy replied.

"Tell us your name, son," Officer Wilson insisted.

The boy's eyes spit daggers, but he spoke up. "I'm Daniel."

"Daniel who?"

"Lane," he muttered.

"Daniel Lane, huh?" Officer Wilson said. "You're Simon and Lily Lane's son."

"Wait, I've seen your name on handbills and posters around town," Nathan remarked. "You're a missing person."

Daniel now refused to make eye contact with any of them.

"All you had to do was knock on the door and tell me you were hungry," Mary said softly.

"And have you hand me over to the police?" Daniel shot back.

"Well, son, get up. You're coming with me," Officer Wilson said.

"I ain't comin' with you!" Daniel cried.

The officer reached down and grabbed his arm, pulling him to his feet. "Sorry. But you don't have any choice." He glanced at Mary. "You all right now, miss?"

"I'm fine." She looked at Daniel's face in the stream of light from the officer's flashlight. "Be careful with him, won't you?"

"Duly noted," the officer said, carting the wriggling boy to his patrol car.

"I'll be happy to make some nice hot tea, if anyone cares for any," Mary declared. "It's awful cold out here, and I'm chilled to the bone."

"No thanks, I need to be heading off," Mr. Zook said.

"So do we," Sam said. He gently grasped Mary's arm. "You are all right now, aren't you?"

"To think that I was terrified of what could be out here, and it was just a frightened, hungry *Englisch* boy," Mary said.

"Often our fears are bigger than the actual danger," Sam replied sagely. "I'm grateful we got the matter sorted before I leave tomorrow. I couldn't bear the thought of you alone and afraid."

"Thank you, Sam. For everything."

Chapter Eleven

Two days later, Mary packed her clothes and got ready to leave. Sam had arranged for Nathan to move in to take care of the Friesen's farm so Mary could go home to be with her family over Christmas, and she felt a mingled sense of relief and sadness.

"Goodbye, Fluffy," she whispered to the cat. Then she went out to the chicken coop, the stable and the cow shed, and bid farewell to all her charges. She'd already bid Sam farewell the day before, and she was already missing him deeply.

Her father arrived by and by, and Mary climbed into his buggy and rode away from the Friesens' farm. She felt a pang of apprehension that she might never see Sam Friesen again, but he had promised to visit her. Mary had his mobile phone number scrawled across her memory—not that she would ever use it now.

Arriving home brought more mixed feelings. Anna and Jacob seemed relieved to have their daughter back, and Mary's sisters were overjoyed at her return. But her heart was now with Sam Friesen, and all she could think of was him. As she set her suitcase down in her bedroom, she thanked God that she could think of Lucy with less guilt, and a greater sense of acceptance. But now a formidable task awaited her – to talk to her father about Sam's desire to court her formally. Sam had said he would ask her father, but she wanted to broach the subject with him first.

"Why didn't you tell us you were afraid to stay on your own?" Anna Lapp asked, coming into Mary's bedroom. "Tell us all about the boy who hid in the Friesen's barn. Everyone from Dovetail to Cedarwood is talking about it and mentioning that you were helpful in catching him."

Mary shook her head. "There were so many of us that night," she replied, thinking of Sam close beside her, "and all I really did was trip the boy with my foot."

"You're a brave girl, Mary, and I'm proud of you. But now, I wish we hadn't sent you away in the first place. We certainly never expected anything like that to happen," Anna remarked.

"It was the right thing, *Mamm*," Mary replied slowly, knowing she was speaking the absolute truth. "I'm glad I had the experience of being on my own and taking care of myself. And I made friends. Mr. Zook and his wife Susan, even Officer Wilson...and Sam Friesen."

"That's *gut* to hear, daughter. I'm glad you think it was a good thing. I was beginning to feel guilty that we had put you through more trauma – what with all those noises you kept hearing each night."

Mary laughed. It certainly hadn't taken long for the gossip mill to reach her parents. "Nobody believed that I was hearing anything at first," she said.

"I'm sorry, Mary," her mother replied.

"Don't be. You know, there was only one person who believed me the whole time, and that was Sam Friesen. Sam gave me a lot of strength through it all."

Anna gave Mary a shrewd look. "You and Sam Friesen seem to have developed a bond of sorts."

Mary took a deep breath. "*Mamm*, I have to talk to *Daed*. Sam Friesen wishes to court me."

Her mother flinched. "The Friesens are Mennonites, Mary. How can you even consider Sam as a prospective mate?"

"This wasn't something we planned," Mary said quietly. "It

came out of the blue, but so gently and naturally that we couldn't help ourselves."

"We sent you to the Friesens to be occupied with a job, earn a small income, and have a change of scenery...not to become involved with someone who is not from our district," her mother said with a good deal of passion.

"*Mamm*, I did everything that you sent me to the Friesens' farm to do. I worked, I earned an income, and I had a change of scenery. But maybe the *gut* Lord had an additional plan for my stay there."

"How could you say that?" Anna scolded. "Mennonites and Amish—"

"...are two sides of the same coin," Mary interjected. "I believe *Gott* gave me Sam who, through all my trials and turmoil during my time at the Friesens' farm, stood by me like a pillar of strength."

"I would say *Gott* was your pillar of strength...not this boy Sam," Anna retorted.

"Anyway, I wish to ask your permission, and *Daed's*, to be courted by Sam," Mary said firmly. "He's away at his university now, but he'll be back."

"He's at a university? Doesn't he work a farm like a good member of our district would? Or what is his trade? What does he even do in university?"

"He's learning modern organic farming techniques," Mary replied. "Because he wishes to take over his parents' farm – since they are now considering staying on in Pennsylvania with Mr. Friesen's elderly parents."

"Oh," Anna said with a sigh. "But he's a Mennonite. They have electricity. Did you use it while you were there?"

Mary shook her head. "No, *Mamm*. Mr. Zook, who is also a Mennonite, brought me lanterns to use."

"They have telephones," Anna said with a look of censure.

"Which I never used...until I had to use one to call Sam and Mr. Zook when the sounds in the night got too much to bear alone," Mary replied. "That telephone brought help in minutes, and we were able to catch the runaway boy."

"Your father will never approve," Anna said finally.

Chapter Twelve

Mary slipped into the telephone shanty and dialed Sam's number from memory. But no matter how many times she called, his cell phone kept ringing, and there was no answer.

"I've been deceived," Mary said to herself, crestfallen. "Sam didn't ever intend to court me. He was probably just trifling with my emotions. Otherwise, why isn't he answering?"

The memory of their supper at the Diner's Delight came back and Mary shook her head.

"Sam couldn't possibly have been pretending," she said aloud. She dialed his number again but got no reply. Then she began to panic – imagining something had happened to him. She imagined him lying on the side of the road with his cell phone flung yards away, where he couldn't get to it. First, she lost Lucy. Now, she had lost Sam, too. She was no good for anybody. The merest contact with her brought only death and devastation. She began to weep – the tears falling all over the telephone receiver.

You're borrowing trouble, she scolded herself. *Enough of this. Enough.*

She dried her eyes and exited the shanty. She would go to Dovetail Village – on the pretext of taking Christmas goodies to the Zooks and the Shrocks, and look for Sam, she decided. He should have returned again from university by now for Christmas.

She hurried home, spurred on by the plan she had. The following day was Christmas Eve. It would be the perfect time to go, and it would only take a few hours. She would ask Sarah or Becky to accompany her. Surely, *Mamm* wouldn't mind.

Mary was so deep in thought that she flew into her house by the side entrance without even noticing the buggy parked on the far side of the driveway. A buggy that she would not have recognized.

"Mary," she heard Sam say, as she collided with him in the hallway on her way toward the kitchen.

"Sam?" Mary breathed. "What are you doing?"

"You've been crying. Is everything not all right?"

She looked around. Her family was in the front room. "I tried to telephone you," she said softly. "And you didn't answer your phone."

"Oh Mary, I'm sorry," he said. "My cell phone battery died on the way here, and I couldn't charge it. I drove a buggy here. Your parents know I'm Mennonite, but I thought the buggy would be less offensive than a car."

Mary stared at him.

"Aren't you going to ask me why I'm here?" he queried, smiling at her.

"What are you doing here?" she asked. Of course, she guessed, but she was deeply nervous that perhaps she was mistaken.

"Your *Daed* was going to take my buggy around to the barn for my horse to be fed, and I said I would do it myself if he pointed me in the right direction," Sam replied. "I was on my way outside when I saw you running through the gate looking distressed."

"And then I ran right into you," Mary whispered, with a smile. "Oh Sam, I'm so glad to see you." She stepped back and stared at him. "You look different," she remarked. "You're dressed like a Mennonite, more plain."

"I'd best take the buggy round to the barn," Sam said, not replying to Mary's remark, but flashing her an enigmatic smile.

"If *Daed* asked you to take your horse to the barn, or offered to do it for you, it can only mean one thing – that you're staying for a bit?"

"Just a few hours, Mary," Sam replied. "I need to get back to the farm so that Nathan can get home for Christmas."

"I see," Mary said, her mind whirling. "I almost hoped you would spend Christmas Day with us...since you will be on your own."

"I need to speak with your *daed* before anything else," he told her.

"I've told *Mamm*...so she has probably already told *Daed*, but I can't be sure."

"I won't be shunned," Mary said.

"*Nee*, child, you won't be," Jacob Lapp replied. "You haven't yet joined church."

"I was going to join last year...and then after Lucy..." Mary said, leaving her sentence incomplete.

"*Jah*, you were taking time to get over the tragedy before you joined the church, and then in the meantime, you went to the Friesens," Anna Lapp mused aloud, her voice tinged with disappointment.

"So, you and *Mamm*, Sarah, Becky and Rachel, will be allowed to maintain contact with me?" Mary asked her father.

"Of course," Jacob replied.

"Mr. Lapp...Mrs. Lapp..." Sam began. "I'm ever so sorry for causing you any grief or uneasiness over this issue, but it was as if the good Lord himself arranged for this to happen, and we were powerless to resist. I promise to be a good husband to Mary, if our courtship develops in that way. As far as I'm concerned, she is the first girl I will be courting and the last. I knew from the moment we met that I had found the most special girl in the world. I want to spend my life with her."

Jacob Lapp gave Mary a serious look. "Mary, my child, do you feel the same as Sam does?"

"*Daed*, you know Sam is the first man in my life, and I know he will be the only one. If I will not be shunned by our district and will be allowed to maintain contact with you all, then... *Ach, Daed,* please give me your permission to accept Sam's courtship."

Jacob looked from Sam to Mary and back again.

"Sam helped me overcome my sorrow and guilt over Lucy," Mary said appealingly. "And I am happy when I am with him."

"You are our eldest child, Mary," Jacob said.

"I know, *Daed*, and I expect you would have liked me to marry someone from our district, but consider this − Sam isn't very far different from us. Nor are any of the Mennonites that I met and became friends with."

"And you say you won't consider the courtship of any man other than Sam Friesen?" Jacob asked Mary.

"Have I ever considered anyone's courtship, *Daed?*" Mary asked, smiling now.

Anna gave her husband a resigned look. "You know how many young men asked to court Mary, and she refused, Jacob."

"None of them were right for me," Mary said.

"Though they were all from Cedarwood and all of them were Amish?" Jacob asked.

"*Jah,*" Mary declared firmly. "There is only one man for me, and that is Sam Friesen."

"I can't believe you've been allowed to court me," Mary said, looking up into Sam's eyes.

"And I can scarce believe I'm at a Nativity Play in a proper Amish barn with Shoofly Pie to follow," Sam declared right back.

He gazed tenderly into her eyes. "I love you so much, Mary. I know we've only been courting formally for a day, and this is hardly the place to ask you, but maybe it is the most appropriate place, after all – will you marry me?"

Mary glowed. Her thoughts flew to Lucy, and she imagined her little sister, standing in front of a Christmas tree, smiling at her.

"I will marry you, Sam," she said. "I will."

The End

Continue Reading...

Thank you for reading ***Missing Lucy at Christmas!*** **Are you wondering what to read next?** Why not read ***Amish Caretaker.*** **Here's a peek for you:**

Norma Glick tried her best to suppress a feeling of quiet pride as she set the tin of shoofly pie down beside the other desserts that members of her community had laid out on the long tables in the Fisher barn. The delicious scent of the molasses-flavored treat was as sweet as it was simple, although Norma knew the amount of labor involved in making it because it was not only her handiwork, but also her own recipe. She stepped back, admiring her pie even though she knew she shouldn't be prideful.

"Mmm." Her youngest brother, Ruben, butted into her reverie. "That smells so *gut*."

"Shoo, Ruben!" Norma laughed. "It's not just for you. Besides, you tasted the filling while I was making it."

"*Jah*, go away, Ruben," boomed a sturdy voice, and Norma's oldest brother playfully shoved Ruben aside. Abel winked at her, his eyes twinkling, and reached toward the pie dish. "This pie is too *gut* for the likes of you."

"Hey!" said Ruben, indignantly. "That's not true."

"This pie is meant to be savored." Abel leaned over it and took a long sniff. "Not just gulped down the way you eat, *brudder*."

Norma slapped Abel's hands away and brandished a dishcloth at all three of her brothers. "I'm warning you, I'll never bake for you again if you keep on like this."

Even though they knew this was an empty threat, Norma's brothers – Ruben, Abel, and the middle brother, Thaddeus – gave her a big-eyed look. Norma laughed. Ruben was the youngest at seventeen, but they all looked like naughty schoolboys.

"You'll have your share when everyone has settled down to the meal," she said.

Ruben's attention had already made its way to the other side of the throng of Amish people making their way out of the Fisher house, where the church service had been held in their meeting room, and toward the barn for the post-service meal. Thaddeus gave his brother a playful elbow.

"Who do you see, Ruben?" he asked.

Ruben turned scarlet. "No one," he said.

Thaddeus laughed, grabbing his brother's arm. "Come on – let's go and talk to her. I mean, let's go and talk to *no one*."

"*Nee*," protested Ruben, but it was no good. Thaddeus was towing him determinedly through the crowd, and Norma could only laugh and shake her head. She turned to Abel. "Where's Beulah today?"

VISIT HERE To Read More!

http://www.ticahousepublishing.com/amish-miller.html

Thank you for Reading

If you **love Amish Romance**, **Visit Here**

https://amish.subscribemenow.com/

to find out about all **New Hannah Miller Amish Romance Releases!** **We will let you know as soon as they become available!**

If you enjoyed *Missing Lucy at Christmas!* would you kindly take a couple minutes to leave a positive review on Amazon? It only takes a moment, and positive reviews truly make a difference. I would be so grateful! Thank you!

Turn the page to discover more Hannah Miller Amish Romances just for you!

More Amish Romance from Hannah Miller

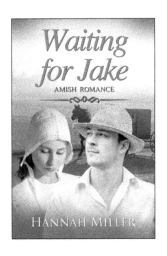

Visit HERE for Hannah Miller's Amish Romance

https://ticahousepublishing.com/amish-miller.html

About the Author

Hannah Miller has been writing Amish Romance for the past seven years. Long intrigued by the Amish way of life, Hannah has traveled the United States, visiting different Amish communities. She treasures her Amish friends and enjoys visiting with them. Hannah makes her home in Indiana, along with her husband, Robert. Together, they have three children and seven grandchildren. Hannah loves to ride bikes in the sunshine. And if it's warm enough for a picnic, you'll find her under the nearest tree!

CPSIA information can be obtained
at www.ICGtesting.com
Printed in the USA
BVHW051142151119
563967BV00010B/67/P

9 781705 496459